AF442138

Franz Kafka: The Life and Legacy of One of the 20th Century's Most Influential Writers

By Charles River Editors

About Charles River Editors

Charles River Editors is a boutique digital publishing company, specializing in bringing history back to life with educational and engaging books on a wide range of topics. Keep up to date with our new and free offerings with this 5 second sign up on our weekly mailing list, and visit Our Kindle Author Page to see other recently published Kindle titles.

We make these books for you and always want to know our readers' opinions, so we encourage you to leave reviews and look forward to publishing new and exciting titles each week.

Introduction

"I write differently from what I speak, I speak differently from what I think, I think differently from the way I ought to think, and so it all proceeds into deepest darkness." – Kafka

In the waning years of the 19th century, Europe began to feel the effects of the Industrial Revolution. With the rise of mechanical technologies that upgraded productivity in terms of raw quantity, the Romantic era was rendered dispensable, and soon to be replaced. The region known as Bohemia, later to be reorganized into the Czech Republic, was buffeted by various influences of the Austrian-Hungarian Empire and the nearby sensibilities of Russian society.

The arts, particularly in the city of Prague, were shaped and reshaped by the pull of nearby Vienna and the European tastes of St. Petersburg. In the previous century, the young Mozart had once called Prague his favorite center of European music. Catherine the Great recreated the artistic splendors of Western cities within proximity to Bohemia, and in the 19th century, composer Antonin Dvorak and others came to represent the final years of the Romantic era in the new state of Czechoslovakia. With the continent's new industrial personality, the arts shed their preoccupation with the importance of personal urges and gave way to a cooler, bare view of life. Programmatic music and realistic art lost their preeminence, and in the more abstract, surreal, and "practical" era that followed, mirroring the effects of mechanical invention, the great writers followed suit.

These changes were naturally reflected in the formation of communistic and fascist societies where factories became the artist's forest, and in tandem with that, imaginations of the heart as artistic expression were abandoned for the embryonic exploration of the mind. Sigmund Freud, born in Freiberg in 1856, captured the fascination of the continent with his theories of the brain's inner workings, and creative writers did the same. The neuroses formulated by the early psychiatrist were imposed on the population as uniformly accurate mental maps for the collective. Where the individual once stood at the center of the equation, the masses took on an extensive code of shared personality symbols against a grey, harsh backdrop, all subsumed within the human dream life.

Among the most engaged of these "surreal" authors was Franz Kafka, only two years Freud's junior. As a Jewish German-language writer, he proved to be an ideal conduit for his era's deepest anxieties. Already emotionally damaged, he was physically weak as well, unable to confront society on any level. His sense of intimidation at the hands of his family reached deeply pathological proportions, and he suffered further from a simultaneous, desperate mix of embrace and revulsion with the Jewish faith. Retreating into familiar representations of his time, Kafka created a series of nightmarish short stories and novels, in which someone much like him played the central role. Settings tended to be a mixture of landmarks, and rather than being based on real events from his life, Kafka's stories are more linked to the habits of his own inner demons and exterior relationships.

Kafka's work was unprecedented in its day, but terms commonly used to describe his work today include "absurdist" and "visionary fiction." The former is at times perceived by modern readers as whimsical, but more correctly applies to locales and situations that could not possibly exist or take place. In the latter, Kafka hangs the presiding issues of the piece on fictitious human and natural riddles that exacerbate the victimhood of central characters. These artificial dilemmas stand as the unsolvable barriers that lace each narrative.

Nearly a century after his death, Kafka is considered one of the greatest writers of the 20th century, despite being a virtual unknown throughout his life. In fact, Kafka never intended for his unpublished work to be released posthumously, but his wishes were ignored, and it was certainly to the world's benefit. Kafka's work is so profound and unique that the term "Kafkaesque" is now a part of the English language, a reference to surreal distortions and amazing complexities, and his works served as the forerunners for some of the 20th century's most influential short forms, such as *The Alfred Hitchcock Hour* and *The Twilight Zone*.

Franz Kafka: The Life and Legacy of One of the 20th Century's Most Influential Writers examines his short life, unique work, and enduring reputation. Along with pictures and a bibliography for further reading, you will learn about Kafka like never before.

Kafka's Early Life

"I cannot make you understand. I cannot make anyone understand what is happening inside me. I cannot even explain it to myself." - Kafka

Franz Amshel (Amshil) Kafka was born in Prague, the central city of Bohemia, on July 3, 1883. He was the son of a merchant named Hermann Kafka, who operated a haberdashery in the retail industry, featuring both men's and women's clothing. His mother was Julie Löwy, a sophisticated woman of extraordinary education for her era, and significantly more advanced than her husband in cultural terms. By the time of their son's birth, the Kafka's had become a prosperous middle class Jewish family.

Kafka's parents

Hermann Kafka, aware of his wife's gifts, desired to place his family within a more prestigious circle than could be found in his village of Wossek some distance from Prague. Further, poverty was endemic to the rural region. With the family's relocation to city life in Prague, he left behind what he viewed as a barbaric way of life and strove to assimilate into a more modern inner city existence. Franz was one of three sons and had three sisters as well, but the older Georg and Heinrich both died when Franz was six. With the resulting alteration of the family dynamic, he was thrust into the position of eldest son, a condition of which he remained intensely conscious for the remainder of his life. Among the three sisters,

Gabriele was born in 1889, Valerie (Ellie) in 1890, and Ottilie (Ottla) in 1892. The youngest remained the closest to him of all the family members.

Kafka's sisters

As part of the assimilation process into an honorable Prague circle, Hermann insisted that his children observe the smallest details of their native Jewish faith. He professed little to no interest in Judaism himself, but the appearance of devotion was essential to social and economic connections. In retrospect, Franz recalled being repulsed by the artificiality surrounding his first Passover, which he termed "a farce."[1] Surpassing that was a lengthy period of apprehension leading up to his bar mitzvah, an

---

[1] Matthew Roth, Franz Kafka, the 20th Century's Realest Surrealist, Jewish Learning – www.myjewishlearning.com/article/franz-kafka/

event that "triggered intense episodes of fear and anxiety."[2] He gave an unusually short speech and suffered through what he perceived as an entirely inconsequential party, later declaring that he "detested it all."[3]

The image-conscious Hermann, who subsequently became a central subject in much of his son's future work, dominated every facet of his children's lives with a harsh and unpredictably volatile temper. Julie Löwy, on the other hand, was a study in contrast. Reared in a family preoccupied with a higher level of intellectualism and a deeper view of spirituality, her father was a merchant and brewer. With an interest in academic society and advanced Judaic concepts, she possessed an all-around cultural richness in which her husband took no interest. Lamentably, she "shared her son's delicate nature,"[4] and she was as dominated by him as the other family members. In this environment, which prevented her from being able to fully interact with her son's education, Julia saw to it that someone fed his intellectual curiosity whenever possible, so by the time he went to school, Franz had secretly spent much of his childhood under the tutelage of governesses and servants. Still, learning was difficult, as he navigated a course of physical and emotional illnesses, due in part to his relationship with the

[2] Matthew Roth

[3] Matthew Roth

[4] IMDB, Franz Kafka Biography – www.imdb.com/name/nm0434525/bio?ref=nm_ov_bio_sin

patriarch.

Exterior stress was a constant as well. By 1890, when he was seven, more than 954,000 Jews lived in the entire region of Bohemia. Waves of pogroms were launched against the Jewish population by both Czech and German nationalists in 1899, and the family became accustomed to being used as "scapegoats,"[5] as others had been throughout Europe. It was in that year that Franz began his formal private schooling. Since his father was indifferent to the entire idea, it was his mother's efforts that sustained him in a system designed for those of considerably greater wealth.

From the beginning, the young Kafka identified not only with his mother, but with her maternal ancestors as well. Generations of them were noted for their spirituality, "intellectual distinction, piety and rabbinical learning."[6] He was drawn to a general state of melancholy common to the women of his family tree, a common feature of their collective disposition, delicate physical frames, and fragile mental constitutions. However, no matter how connected to his mother as he may have been, it was not possible for him to share a closeness with her because she was subservient to a husband prone to raging and "exacting business"[7] at all times. In particular, Hermann

---

[5] May Benatar, Psychotherapist, author, Kafka and the Doll: The Pervasiveness of Loss, HuffPost, Dec. 3. 2011

[6] Encyclopaedia Britannica, Franz Kafka, German Language Writer – www.britannica.com/biography/Franz-Kafka

[7] Encyclopaedia Britannica

took an immediate dislike to his son's unprofitable and unhealthy dedication to recording the details of his "dreamlike inner life."[8] His "coarse, practical, [and] domineering"[9] presence took root in the boy's imagination, transforming him into one of a race of giants. Later describing his father as a "repulsive tyrant,"[10] Kafka failed to ever confront his father, departing at last from his family home only after decades of suffering and preferring to live with a broken will.

In his later novels, none of which were completed but are now famous nonetheless, the "giant" of his childhood appeared in an increasingly grander scale. The wall between the two was transferred to all other humans as the author believed that his greatest terrors could be avoided by "ultimate isolation."[11] The wall against intimacy extended to those who could best qualify as an inner circle. This included all the jobs he was too afraid to leave, the friends he cherished in at least an interior sense, the women he loved so erratically, and the institutions of the society in which he lived daily life. Above all, the strongest portion of his wall was reserved for God and the human representatives of his business on Earth. What duty he paid to the brand of Judaism practiced in his family home was perfunctory at best. In the early years, he

---

[8] Encyclopaedia Britannica
[9] Encyclopaedia Britannica
[10] Encyclopaedia Britannica
[11] Encyclopaedia Britannica

maintained a public and private existence in the German language and culture, allowing no other influence to intrude. In his essential business and personal dealings, he remained ever "timid, guilt-ridden, [and] obedient."[12] Physical manifestations of various anxieties included a hypersensitivity to loud noises, but he was not without havens for escape. He participated in sports such as swimming, rowing, and hiking. He also enjoyed the cinema and was an avid fan of Charlie Chaplin, particularly in his role as a hero in *The Kid*.

In his late secondary school years, completed in 1901, Kafka entered into a political immersion in the prevailing tides that would lead to the Russian Revolution and First World War. Developing a sympathy for leftist thought, he regularly attended anarchist meetings and took a special interest in Judaic behavior as a political component of the continent. Despite a new bent for a socialized form of nearly "secular" Zionism, he remained standoffish and detached from actual religious practices. Never prepared to come out as a true firebrand, a lifetime of decorum covered many of his most controversial passions, and he avoided any hint of confrontation with his most problematic individuals.

Kafka's excellent record at the Altstädter Gymnasium for the academic elite smoothed his passage to a higher

---

[12] Encyclopaedia Britannica

level, one of few that he was ever to truly enjoy. He began his first year of university in 1901 at the Charles University, prominent among the landmarks of the city of Prague. Established in the mid-14th century, it was the oldest in Central Europe.

The palace where Kafka attended gymnasium

After years of personal constriction, he found himself flourishing in a "dehumanized humanistic curriculum."[13] During the first two weeks of class, he was officially listed as a chemistry major, which was not entirely at odds with his father's wishes. However, when he switched to law in the third week, the senior Kafka was nearly

---

[13] Encyclopaedia Britannica

ecstatic. For centuries, the study of law had been a ubiquitous choice among European families for their sons, particularly in the Austrian Empire. Steeped in an academic regimen, Kafka felt less friction with his father's frivolous demands for a pious appearance and his obsession with connections. He soon declared himself to be both an atheist and a socialist. What Kafka's father failed to realize was that declaring a specialty in law put his son in constant contact with a culture steeped in writing and debates, both legal and political. Further, it took Franz ever nearer to his abiding interest in general arts and literature. As a great if not temporary relief, the legal arena relocated religion as mere fodder for analytical rigor rather than a life pact made with the other world.

Metamorphosis

"A non-writing writer is a monster courting insanity." - Kafka

After five years of free reign for his personal thoughts without immediate paternal censorship, Kafka's law degree was completed in 1906, and from that moment, the youthful joy of sorting out the universe through lofty conceptual logic and rhetorical flourish ended. Kafka spent the following year in the customary way for a law student as an unpaid clerk. Such drudgery led to a situation that for Kafka afforded little joy, a regimen of work for the insurance industry. His increasingly powerful urge to write was blunted by an exhaustive schedule imposed upon an already fragile employee.

Kafka in 1906

Through a series of acquaintances, Kafka found himself working in the Prague branch of the Italian Assicurazioni Generali. The recommendation came from Arnold Weissberger, a U.S. Vice Consul who returned to Prague as the chief clerk at a major bank. Kafka envisioned the opportunity as the "fulfillment of his exotic dream,"[14] and

<hr>

[14] Franz Kafka Museum, Franz Kafka, Assicurazioni Generali – www.kafkamuseum.cz/en/franz-kafka/employment/assicurazioni-generali/

upon assuming he would be posted in Trieste, he began to study Italian. He would instead suffer through a series of disappointments, the first of which was a posting in Prague. All in all, the position proved to be a "terrible fit."[15]

Installed in the life insurance division, any thoughts of relocating far from family were dashed. Life insurance was in virtually all cases handled by local employees, and his new office was located at Wenceslas Square and Jindrisska Street. Kafka grew instantly disenchanted with the working conditions and a schedule based on the "double-shift system."[16] This entailed a lengthy workday of 8 am to 6 pm with a two-hour break at noon. One could apply for a two-week leave once every two years. No outside employment was allowed without written permission from the company, and no honorary offices could be held during one's term of employment. An initial period of probation took up the first year, and the company could require unpaid overtime, despite already mediocre wages. Kafka had intended to preserve his evenings for writing, but the exhaustion accumulated through a single day of work rendered that unworkable. He remained with the company for less than one year, through July of 1908. In retrospect, he cited little else than bad memories with the Italian company, with the exception of an acquaintance formed with director Ernst

[15] Biography, Franz Kafka, Author (1883-1924) April 2, 2014 – www.biography.com/writer/franz-kafka
[16] Franz Kafka Museum, Assicurazioni Generali

Eisner, a literature afficionado.

A picture of the building where Kafka worked

Transferring to another insurance company with virtually no delay, Kafka found himself at the Worker's Accident Insurance Institute for the Kingdom of Bohemia through a similar set of indirect connections. He was recommended by college friend Ewald Felix Pribram, whose father had served as Secretary to the organization. With an improved set of conditions, Kafka was to remain there for a period of 14 years, much of it spent as the boss's right-hand-man. The excellence of Kafka's performance was self-evident. Within two years, he became a permanent civil servant, and within five years, he was a junior secretary to the most important insurance organization in Austria. After 12 years, he went on to become a secretary, going on to Senior Secretary two years later.

The more humane conditions Kafka found there enabled him to make good on life-long aspirations as a writer, and the industry that provided his livelihood inadvertently shaped his writing style as well. The requirements of an insurance writer required the skillful use of "formal, cold language"[17] that served as such an asset to his stark story lines. Avoiding sentimentality in the interpretations of his characters, that responsibility was transferred to the readers, whose imaginations can run a great deal farther than the most adroit written descriptions. Kafka's construction of relationships between protagonists and antagonists is in every case unequal - the standard equation for the premise is invariably one of transgression and punishment, perpetrator and victim, "domination and submission."[18] Considering the small output Kafka produced in his short life, his obsession for any opportunity to write in seclusion bordered on the

---

[17] IMDB. Biography

[18] Anna Katherina Schaffner, Masochism: Franz Kafka and the Evolution of Suffering, Springer – www.link.springer.com/chapter/10.1057/9780230358904_10

maniacal, overriding all other considerations considered prerequisite by the outer world. As he put it, "All I am is literature, and I am not able or willing to be anything else."[19]

While he famously claimed that books were nothing short of a narcotic, he was oddly unable to complete a single novel, and the only published works of any length were short story collections. Allen Thiher described Kafka's early experimentations with fiction writing as a search for "voice, theme, and orientation."[20] Youthful works in all arts generally go through both initial awkwardness and daring creativity, and the fretful "venting" of Kafka stories would not be tamed through the years, but smoothed and unfurled in a more sage-like manner without losing the raw power so inherent to his entire output.

The first publication of Kafka's work came near the end of 1908 in Hamburg through *Hyperion* magazine. Eight of the early short stories were published as the first *Hyperion* publications, while five more pieces appeared in the newspaper *Bohemia* in the following year. All were published into book form entitled *Betrachtung (Meditations)* two years later.

---

[19] Anna Katharina Schaffner

[20] Allen Thiher, Kafka's Early Experiments in Writing Fiction, from *Understanding Franz Kafka*, 1018, University of South Carolina Press

These were short stories written in the preceding years, sharing the common themes of uncertainty, traveling into unfamiliar locations with contrarian rules, and dream states. Characters typically make minute observations on their journeys that lead to new knowledge of the world and self. For example, "Children on a Country Road" depicts the night-time dream life of a young girl who journeys into the woods where children play king-of-the-hill. Girls are pushed into ditches, and she learns of a village where no one ever sleeps. In that dreamscape, she receives her first kiss. In other stories, dreamlike companions are unmasked as "tricksters," and business is revealed as the vehicle by which one loses his soul. Continuing with common themes Kafka associated with his own personal despair, "The Sudden Walk" describes a character's leap to enlightenment that separates him at last from a family he believes is doomed to oblivion. "Excursions into the Mountains" is a flight from a seemingly immovable reality, while "Bachelor's Ill Luck" is an essay on loneliness, where the character feels required to explain his lack of children or life partner. "On the Tram" is one of many examples in which the author views young women from a distance and questions his purpose in being there. That theme is also central to "The Rejection", an imagined conversation with a woman who expresses no interest in him. "The Wish to Be a Red Indian" employs the western figure as a symbol of freedom, and a haven from his life of social repression. In "The Trees", humans are compared to immobile tree trunks which must inevitably fall down.

During this time, magazines and newspapers such as *Hyperion* became the "dominant genre"[21] of the café culture in the major cities of Paris, Berlin, and Vienna. The coffee house was the meeting place for writers, artists, and intellectuals, and since the majority of visitors only had limited hours for reading, the sidewalk offerings were most often miniatures, leaving full novels to publishers. In German-speaking Prague, a rich slate of public lectures was offered, and young writers found their way onto the podiums for public readings. Never able to complete a novel, it seems these miniatures were the only genres in which Kafka was entirely comfortable, though others have argued that his misfortune with novels is due simply to time constraints. He gave up early novels such as *Wedding Preparations in the Country* to pen the first short stories, and he habitually did the same with other lengthy projects in order to complete his now iconic sketches.

Kafka's earliest published works were met with criticisms that the fragmented plots had little relevance to waking reality and therefore failed to satisfy literary

---

[21] Judith Ryan, Kafka Before Kafka., The Early Stories, from *A Companion to the Works of Franz Kafka*, NED-New Edition, 2002, Boydell and Brewer, Camden House

norms of development. Among the initial responses was a critique that mocked the stories as "*Seifenblasen*,"[22] or "soap bubbles."

From childhood, Kafka dreamed of visiting exotic places around the globe, and although the fulfillment of his wish was somewhat limited, he was able to tour northern Europe with his closest friend, Max Brod. Brod was a novelist, essayist, and fellow law student who in his later career was to become a minor government official. As a side pursuit, he served as a music and drama critic for the *Prager Tagblatt* newspaper. Recognizing Kafka's gift early on, his greatest importance was to encourage publication of his friend's complete works after his death. That the works of Kafka were passed on to the next generation at all was largely accomplished through Brod's efforts. In a bold decision, he countermanded the author's request that his manuscripts be destroyed upon his death. The principal source of data on Kafka, his works, and writing process, Brod took responsibility for editing his friend's diaries. Further, as an active Zionist from 1912 on, he was an important influence in Kafka's spiritual struggle with Judaism.

On other occasions, Kafka traveled alone, and at one point he participated in a Viennese conference for the

---

[22] James Rolleston, Temporal Space: A Reading of Kafka's "Betrachtung", *Modern Austrian Literature*, Vol. 11, No. 3/4, Special Franz Kafka Issue (1978), Association of Austrian Studies.

insurance industry. The two visited various points of Italy, Paris, and Weimar. He had always been drawn to travel books, designed to glorify the exotic aspects of each location, and as an author, the idea of travel stood as a central "metaphor for the internal process of writing itself."[23]

Kafka in 1910

Unfortunately for Kafka, 1911 offered limited freedom to write, because Kafka spent part of the year as a factory worker in his brother-in-law's asbestos facility. However,

---

[23] Zilcosky, John, Kafka's Travels: Exoticism, Colonialism, and the Traffic of Writing, Reviewed by Christina Gerhardt, TRANSIT – www.transit.berkely7.edu/2006/gerhardt/

the most significant events in his development occurred at
home when he visited a performance of Yiddish theater.
In the last decade of the 19th century, such theater groups,
many hailing from Poland, Hungary, and Bohemia,
crisscrossed Europe in lengthy tours. Inspired by the
techniques of Stanislavski and Brecht, performances were
varied, including operas and operettas, cabaret evenings,
and avant-garde performances. For Kafka, at odds with
the Judaism of his childhood, these offerings brought
Jewish tradition out of the abstract into a potent and
definable environment where he could sense a graspable
identity.

Particularly drawn to a small troupe called the Lemberg
Group, Kafka attended performances at the Café Savoy.
The players pretended to be German, but they had
gathered from all over Europe. At once, the energy and
raw acting style found their way into his stories, with
"dramatic and physically expressive characters."[24] Much
commentary about this troupe can be found in Kafka's
personal diaries, which he kept up with religiously
through his early professional years. In particular, he
seems to have had an obsession with one of the cast's
actresses, Mania Tschissik.

Despite the struggles with new romantic interest Felice

[24] Haffner, Charlotte Yiddish Theater, Franz Kafka and Art Movements of the 20th Century, Jewish Museum London –
www.jewishmuseum.org.uk/2018/1/11/yiddish-theater-franz-kafka-and-art-movements/

Bauer and his own conflicting impulses, the completion of "The Judgment" ushered in a period of high productivity and a fresh energy supplied by his contact with Yiddish theater. In 1912, he offered what was described as a "revelatory"[25] lecture in the Jewish Town Hall of Prague. In this presentation, he raved about the virtues of Yiddish expression in general, a signal of his later Judaism and Zionism. He further declared that once the words, melody and central characteristics of the culture's artistic expression have overcome the beholder, "you will have forgotten your former reserve."[26]

His utter fascination with Yiddish Theater was to be an abiding one, and his tug-of-war between love and isolation was personified by his interest in Yiddish actress Mania Tschissik. A spellbound Kafka had witnessed several of her performances, and he spoke of how she evoked images in his mind of "hybrid"[27] creatures such as sirens and mermaids. Despite his rapt attention to every moment Tschissik spent on the stage, it was essential that he avoid looking directly at her throughout the evening. As he explained, "For that would have meant that I loved her."[28] No actual relationship ever materialized.

In the same year, he made strides with his first novel,

[25] Matthew Roth

[26] Guido Massimo, Franz Kafka's Vagabond Stars, Digital Yiddish Theater Project – www.web-uwm.edu/yiddish-stage/franz-kafkas-vagabond-stars

[27] Guido Massimo

[28] Guido Massimo

Amerika, or The Man Who Disappeared (*Der Verschollene*), which would not be published until many years later in its incomplete form. Following closely after the first published stories, Kafka's central premise revolved around a boy named Karl Rossman who was sent to the New World to negotiate an altered and unfriendly continent. In the story, the young Rossman visits American shores at the insistence of his family after he is seduced by a maid who bears his son. This is explained in an opening short story, "The Stoker", which serves as a first chapter. Among Kafka's favorite books was Benjamin Franklin's autobiography, but the "Amerika" to which Rossman eventually travels is modern and contorted in surreal fashion. Upon the first sighting of New York Harbor, Rossman notes the Statue of Liberty hoists a sword rather than a torch. In his struggles to understand the American way of life, he seeks shelter with several father figures, and he is exploited at every turn by both rich and poor. In the final chapter, Rossman enters a dream world entitled "Nature Theater of Oklahoma", representing a welcome death and afterlife.

The majority of Kafka's protagonists were "confident and energetic"[29] types, at least at the beginning of their stories, but Rossman was uncharacteristically passive, shy, and inexperienced. He is cast into his new dream

---

[29] A Gentleman's Library, Amerika (Franz Kafka): A Summary and Analysis – www.gentleman'slibrary.com/amerika-franz-kafka-summary-and-analysis/

country with no money, stature, or most importantly, a vocation. Of his many trials, the first comes early as he loses a box containing all his possessions upon arrival. Coming under the wing of wealthy Uncle Jacob, he is cast into an environment of utter luxury, but suffers constant exploitation by figures of the aristocratic class and lower-level criminals. His inheritance from Uncle Jacob is endangered by two intrusive companions, and his benefactor later reveals that he possesses the box of items lost in the beginning. In an odd description by an author who never traveled to America, only the occasional European is willing to be of any help, such as the German woman who operates a hotel. Rossman becomes her elevator boy in the naïve belief that hard work directly results in success at all things. Arriving at the "Nature Theater of Oklahoma", he learns that even in the afterlife, vocation is important. As an example, one such as Rossman might aspire to be one of God's angelic trumpeters. However, as it is below in Amerika, one is required to produce his "proper papers,"[30] and the only relief from day-to-day anxiety is to board a train.

Among other patterns that set *Amerika* apart is that it takes place in an actual milieu in a reality-based location. As in Kafka's other works, all is seen through the eyes of a central character, with introspection giving way to

---

[30] A Gentleman's Library

everything out "there"[31] in the exterior world. Kafka makes no claim to a starkly realistic Amerika, but instead uses a fantasy hybrid as a model for social apathy, goal-driven lives, and abuse inflicted upon the stranger in the name of profit. The hybrid setting renders some of the writing rather "wooden"[32] in an attempt to smooth over artificial circumstances. Even Rossman's death in Oklahoma turns out to be a semi-dream state that abandons reality, leaving only a "fragmentary"[33] and confusing existence. In the end, much of *Amerika* comes down to knowing the ropes, being wise to schemes, and establishing one's value through vocation.

Felice Bauer represented one of only a handful of romantic interests in Kafka's life. The two met at Brod's home in 1912, and a five-year relationship ensued, the bulk of it expressed through the postal system between Prague and Berlin. What has been termed a "pen romance"[34] involved few personal encounters during the five years, as the two interacted through a collection of nearly 600 letters between them. Bauer hailed from Upper Silesia, the home of her mother, and her father was Viennese. She worked as a fellow insurance agent, and then at a voice equipment company that manufactured gramophones with a branch in Prague. At the start of the

[31] A Gentleman's Library

[32] A Gentleman's Library

[33] A Gentleman's Library

[34] Franz Kafka Museum, Felice Bauer – www.kafkamuseum.cz/franz-kafka/women/felice-bauer/

First World War, she became increasingly active as a
Zionist, and she volunteered at the Jewish People's Home
in Prague for refugees coming out of Russia. Bauer's
sister Erna and brother Ferry were featured in Kafka's
letters.

Felice has been described as a "capable, practical and
orderly woman"[35] who had somewhat mundane tastes in
comparison to those of her love interest. She possessed
middle-class sensibilities that included little interest in
either art or literature. Still, Kafka admired her
temperament, even if it complicated their relationship
from time to time. Bauer could not understand Kafka's
outward romantic desire for her, nor the battle between his
need for isolation as a writer. According to his written
missives, the author tortured himself between "yearning
for her company versus the need for solitude."[36] Despite
his expressed loneliness in her nearly constant absence, he
made clear his distaste for either cohabitation or physical
contact. Further, he seldom passed up an opportunity to
defend the ideal "monastic"[37] life of a writer, while at the
same time expressing a wish to start a family.

Constantly at odds with themselves and with each other,
the mutual dilemma resulted in two engagement
announcements, one in 1912 and the other five years after.

---

[35] Franz Kafka Museum, Felice Bauer
[36] Franz Kafka Museum, Felice Bauer
[37] Franz Kafka Museum, Felice Bauer

On both occasions, Kafka broke it off immediately and conveniently. Eventually, the standoff could no longer sustain itself, and Bauer married a businessman named Marasse, with whom she raised two children.

In the early months of Kafka's relationship with Bauer, he wrote one of the most autobiographical stories of his career, and in large part he attributed its completion to Bauer, as represented in the principal female character. Important elements of "The Judgment" are corroborated by the author's personal diaries as being drawn directly from his own life, particularly in terms of the difficulties posed by Bauer's presence in his routine. As is usually the case, Hermann Kafka is present as the male character's father.

"The Judgment" was written in one night without a pause. As perspective on the difficulty of dealing with such subject matter, Kafka likens the writing process to that of a newborn child. Male artists have often claimed that their regimen is the closest a man can come to childbirth, and in the case of "The Judgment", he characterized the result as "covered with dirt and mucus as it comes out of him."[38] Despite the rapidity with which the story was written, Kafka returned to it with the intent of fleshing out every ambiguity of relationships not clear

---

[38] CliffsNotes, The Metamorphosis and Other Studies, Summary and Analysis, The Judgment "(Das Urteil)" – www.cliffsnotes.com/literature/m/the-The Metamorphosis-and-otherstories/summary-and-analysis/the-judgment-das-urteil

to him in the original. Although written in a single night, actual completion was to take another three years. Among the most arduous of his works, most of "The Judgment" remained in its original form, and the author recalled that he "carried his own weight on his back more than once that night."[39]

The first meeting with Bauer took place six weeks before "The Judgment" was written, and already the manic dance of seduction and revulsion had begun. "The Judgment" made on the central character "George" by his father was according to one analyst as "inexorable"[40] as Bauer's sudden "weighty" presence to the author. Discussions of the need for bachelorhood contrasted with the desire for a happy family life had already begun, and the dichotomy served as the most important premise of the story, in conjunction with "perfectionist notions of what writing should be,"[41] excluding the romantic partner.

Kafka openly admitted that he was indebted to Bauer for the inspiration, but in the story, George dies because of the female character, Frieda. George's bachelorhood became the archetype of the writer, and the thirst for loneliness, while Bauer's character represented the sensual world. As in his real life, Kafka lived each day under the oppressive cloud of a guilty conscience, typified

---

[39] CliffsNotes
[40] CliffsNotes
[41] CliffsNotes

by the manner in which his character dodges his father's inquiries. In reality, Kafka always accepted his own father's judgments without complaining or questioning. That ongoing failure is said to be represented in the story by George's death by drowning.

"The Metamorphosis" emerged from the same period and was published in 1915, but it certainly represented an advancement in Kafka's writing. The most iconic of all Kafka's short stories, his literary nightmare goes far beyond what many could probably have imagined. Also begun in the first months of Bauer's presence, the shocking story of a man transforming into an insect was written from Kafka's third floor room with a direct view of the Vltava River. The toll bridge below seemed to figure prominently in Kafka's thoughts at the time. In his diary entries for that year, he remarked, "I would stand at the window for long periods…and was frequently tempted to amaze the toll collector on the bridge below on my plunge."[42]

"The Metamorphosis" has been characterized as a "classic analogy of alienation and displacement,"[43] with autobiographical overtones spread throughout the document. The young man Gregor, who is devoted to supporting his family, is not primarily alarmed by his

[42] Biography, Franz Kafka, Author (1883-1924, April 2, 2014 – www.biography.com/writer/franz-kafka

[43] Shmoop, Franz Kafka Timeline – www.schmoop.com/franz-kafka/timeline.html

transformation and indeed "doesn't appear significantly bothered by it."[44] What concerns the victim of nature is the possibility of arriving late at his workplace and losing his familiar comforts, finances, and family. Once discovered, he hides under the sofa in shame. His devoted sister overcomes her initial shock and attempts to care for him by bringing food. However, Gregor feels his tastes changing to only the moldiest of offerings. Hearing his family converse on the other side of the door, he feels proud at having sustained them, for a time thinking both as a human and insect.

The transformation is never explained, and nothing indicates that Gregor merited such a change. His condition is treated as an illness. The family remains united, and only the maid begs to be released due to the supposed uncleanliness that "disturbs the sense of order in the house."[45] Unable to think in two incarnations, the victim gradually behaves more like an insect, although some humanity remains behind. However, his sister eventually concludes that the family must get rid of him.

"The Metamorphosis" is motif-laden, and the transformations are not solely limited to the altered young man. Through his disaster, the family is roused from a condition that is "hopeless and static."[46] They begin to

____

[44] Matthew Roth

[45] Matthew Roth

[46] Matthew Roth

overcome their own problems, and the sister ceases to be a caretaker. Gregor eventually dies, hastened by an attack by his father, but the family is "reinvigorated"[47] by his absence. The patriarch begins to sleep in his uniform, the symbol of his dignity, and the sister matures into a more self-owned person.

During his time as an insect, Gregor does not attain any enlightenment, unlike his family, and is altered further into the way of the insect kingdom. The narrator speaks throughout in the third person in a flat tone, offering no encouragement or color for the reader. The time is unspecified, but it seems to take place in the late 19th century or early 20th century. An example of "absurdist" literature where such things are possible, Gregor's hybrid condition speaks of a disconnect between mind and body, as well as the resulting "limits of sympathy."[48] The same theme of participation and revulsion is present in Nabokov's *Lolita.*

Nina Pelikan Straus takes on "The Metamorphosis" as a feminist, noting that by 1977, 10,000 works about Kafka were in print, nearly all written by men. She also pointed out that every field related to psychoanalysis, philosophy, social and political worlds, and above all Marxism, have found the story "inexhaustible"[49] with so many avenues of

---

[47] Matthew Roth

[48] Matthew Roth

[49] Nina Pelikan Straus, Transforming Franz Kafka's "The Metamorphosis", *Signs*, Vol. 14, No. 3 (Spring 1989) University of

interpretation available. She cited Christian Goode's reference to the story as "a literary Rorschach test."[50] To a feminist, "The Metamorphosis" could deal with European-style female rebellion by the women of the time consigned to being "caretakers and feeders."[51] The sister blooms while the victim of the transformation deteriorates. In this way, she is "pried loose"[52] from the role.

Kafka's sporadic writing continued, and the next work considered important in the Kafka canon is "The Trial", written in 1914 and 1915. The meaning of this tale is described by some as unknowable since it is based on a character's absolute lack of knowledge as to what has happened to him. A young banker who has done nothing wrong is unexpectedly arrested on his 30th birthday, and a year later, he is taken by two men from an unknown court to a quarry outside of town and killed. In the intervening year, he is never informed as to the charges, and he waits outside the doors of an untouchable court,"[53] but he is never allowed to enter and plead his case. He lives and dies in ignorance of his fate.

While the work is certainly unique, it is a reminder that

Chicago Press

[50] Nina Pelikan Straus

[51] Nina Pelikan Straus

[52] Nina Pelikan Straus

[53] Donald M. Kartinager, Job and Joseph K: Myth in Kafka's "The Trial", *Modern Fiction Series* Vol. 8 no. 1, FRANZ KAFKA Special Number (Spring 1962) Johns Hopkins University Press

human beings control less than what they often assume, and the potency of utter helplessness and lack of importance rivals any work of horror. Donald Kartinager ascribed the use of myth to the tale, a case in which unseen other-worldly powers "throw dice" over people's lives. He analogized it to the Book of Job in the Old Testament and the wager between God and his counterpart to prove his subject's loyalty. Kafka was well-versed in the Bible and Talmud, and like Job, Josef K. the protagonist, contends with a miffed deity possessing the larger authority, experience, and universal view. Margaret Church contended that in a father-son relationship steeped in discord, "The Trial" could be seen as an example of "a hero in search of a father."[54] She went on to cite the transformation of time and space to a pliable and illusory reality, dissolving the tenets of known physics.

In this dreamlike existence that serves as a sort of forerunner for the works of Alfred Hitchcock and Rod Serling, the riskiest moment of the day is the moment of awakening. The new day is altered from the evening before, and who knows what might have been tinkered with in the hours between. Josef K. dutifully hurries to court in order to be there by 9:00 a.m., although he has not been instructed to do so. It is his first Sunday in court, and despite being late, he walks slowly due to his abundance

---

[54] Margaret Church, Time and Reality in Kafka's The Trial and The Castle, *Twentieth Century Literature,* Vol. 2 No. 2 (July 1956)

of available time. It is the "dream within a dream" that allows such a loose view of time, and one which can finally determine that perception is not reality, nor is the court itself "real." That realization, however, does not dispel the dread such a situation can mete out to the unknowing victim. Kafka himself cited the influence of Dostoyevsky's *Crime and Punishment* and *The Brothers Karamazov.*

In 1914, Kafka made several changes in his personal life, beginning with the first premarital breakup with Felice Bauer. At the same time, his hands-off courtship of Grete Bloch began. All of this occurred within the onset of World War I, and Kafka spent much free time attending scientific lectures at the home of Berta Fanta, a literary and intellectual figure who attracted such ascending stars as Albert Einstein and Rudolf Steiner to her evening gatherings. In addition to participating, Kafka was thrilled to hear of new concepts in science, including quantum theory, relativity, psychoanalysis, and transfinite numbers. He possessed an intense interest in alternative medicine and modern educational methods like Montessori, as well as technical oddities and aviation. His interest in nutrition attracted him to the Fletcherites, who engaged in a fad instigated by Horace Fletcher to chew one's food into a liquid state before swallowing. Several hundred repetitions were required for the smallest morsel, making meals at the Kafka household a tense experience.

Fanta

In a profound act of courage, however brief, 1914 was also the year in which Kafka moved away from his parents' home for the first time. In his new apartment on Bilkova Street, he worked on several iconic stories, completing "The Trial" and beginning "In the Penal Colony". These offerings are considered by many to be Kafka's best works. Like the main character in "The Trial", "In the Penal Colony" features a character who is not informed or given any avenue of redress or escape. The story is based on four characters: The Condemned Man, The Explorer, The Officer, and The Soldier. Each must "come to grips"[55] with a "machine" built to torture

---

[55] SuperSummary, In the Penal Colony – www.supersummary.com/in-the-penal-colony/

and execute prisoners. It is be used for the first time on
The Condemned Man.

The Explorer arrives to witness the execution, and The
Officer who loves the machine eagerly explains how it
works. The apparatus imprints the commandment that the
victim has violated into his skin. In grotesque fashion, the
body is rotated through rows of needles that complete the
script. "Honor thy superiors" is to be etched into The
Condemned Man, but The Explorer is too horrified by the
prospect and seeks to end the exercise. Talking The
Officer out of the practice, The Condemned Man is set
free. The Officer proceeds to sit in the machine instead,
with the selected script, "Be just." However, the machine
malfunctions and impales him. The surviving members
subsequently head to a tea shop, where they discuss the
incident and part company.

As with all Kafka works, interpretations of the work are
quite varied. Doreen Fowler drew a parallel between the
harsh Old Testament and the milder doctrines of the New
Testament. When The Explorer declines to participate in
the violence, The Officer responds, "Then the time has
come."[56] The machine, the old order, responds to guilt,
and its discontinued use for Fowler marked the death of
the old theology.

---

[56] Doreen F. Fowler, "In the Penal Colony": Kafka's Unorthodox Theology, *College Literature* Vol. 6 no. 2, CEA Increment
(Spring, 1979), Johns Hopkins University Press

A more literal and secular view is held by Heinz Politzer, who referred to the machine as "the tortures to which Kafka the writer has subjected himself."[57] Walter Sokel's take differed in that it ascribed the story to a response against the most enduring personal problem, his father - "as always."[58] Wilhelm Emrich placed the work's meaning at the feet of the largest dilemma of life: the approach of death. This is The Condemned Man's "ultimate (absolute) catastrophe."[59] Others attach a deep meaning to the author's attack on official authority and society's surrender to fascism. In the more personal realm, the specter of "the machine" embodies "sublimations of the pangs of tuberculosis or sexual impotency."[60]

Upon completion of the work, Kafka found himself at odds with an editor who urged him to change the title to "In the Gangster Colony", based on supposed marketability. Kafka was probably correct to defend the original moniker, since a gangster attack is simply an intrusion of evil intent that eliminates the mechanism of judgment, trial, and institutional authority.

In this period, Kafka may have been at the highest state of awareness in his life as to the works of fellow authors in his genre. Unique as his mature works may be, readers

---

[57] Kurt J. Fickert, A Literal Interpretation of "In the Penal Colony", *Modern Fiction Studies* Vol. 17, no. 1. Special Number the Modern German Novel (Spring, 1971), Johns Hopkins University Press

[58] Kurt. J. Fickert

[59] Kurt J. Fickert

[60] Kurt J. Fickert

may find literary connections to Edgar Allen Poe, E.T.A. Hoffmann, and Nikolai Gogol, in addition to cultural collections such as the Bible, Talmud, and Chinese parables.

Kafka's Final Years

"Man cannot live without a permanent trust in something indestructible within himself, though both that indestructible something and his own trust in it may remain permanently concealed from him." - Kafka

By 1916, Kafka had relocated once more, renting a room in Golden Lane, a quaint street within Prague Castle dotted with small houses. During his time there, he penned "A Country Doctor" and "A Report to an Academy". In a dreamscape only a serious psychoanalyst would attempt to untangle in terms of symbolism, the country doctor is called to a patient 10 miles away in the middle of winter. His horse dies, but a mysterious groom appears with a pair of horses. They take him to the patient, but as he departs, he sees the groom making advances on his maid. He cannot rescue her or speak at all because he is in the man's debt, and the horses will not turn regardless. The patient is a bedridden boy with no ailment, yet he begs the doctor to let him die. When an infection of "multi-legged worms"[61] is found on his side, the patient

---

[61] Hans P. Guth, Symbol and Contextual Restraint: Kafka's "Country Doctor," *PMLA*, Vol. 80 no. 4 (Sep., 1965) Modern Language Association

changes his mind. In a conflict with the family that sings a
"quasi-religious verse,"[62] the doctor is stripped and put in
bed with the patient to cure him. He tells the boy that the
infection is not lethal, grabs his clothes, and climbs back
in the carriage, still naked. On the cold ride home, he fears
the loss of his practice and worries about the fate of his
maid at the hands of the groom.

According to Hans Guth, the doctor symbolizes the "I"
or "Id" who cannot reach his goal, and the treatment
received at the hands of the family is betrayal by those he
deems to be lesser beings than himself. This is perhaps a
rare flash of ego on Kafka's part, and a revelation that
those who are overly humble about their work are at times
the most egotistical of all, devoting much energy to
resisting discovery. The doctor shares a quality of
"paradoxical gallantry"[63] that at times reads as "pathetic
bravado."[64]

When Kafka was diagnosed with tuberculosis in 1917,
Brod recommended that he pay a visit to specialist
Professor Friedel Pick, who examined him and took x-
rays. The diagnosis was "apical lesions," to which Kafka
responded, "That's like calling someone a piglet when
you really mean swine."[65] The illness forced him to retire

---

[62] Hans P. Guth

[63] Hans P. Guth

[64] Hans P. Guth

[65] Vitalis, Franz Kafka's World, Kafka's Illness – www.vitalis-verlag.com/en/topics/kafkas-world/kafkas-krankheit/

from his work with Worker's Insurance. Whether it forced or enabled him to disconnect from Felice Bauer for a second and final time is unclear. However, many theorize that he used his condition not to rid himself of her, but rather of the affection and emotional proximity she might represent. Either way, the two went their separate ways.

That same year, Kafka moved again, this time to an apartment in Lesser Town of Prague, a historic district. The building he lived in now houses the U.S. embassy. During this time, he wrote "The Great Wall of China". An unconventional work lacking clear plot progression, the story embodies "the musings of a nameless narrator"[66] who took part in its construction. The wall is in the end only a starting point. From the backstory of the worker, who is a supervisor, the character is geographically and personally irrelevant to the emperor he serves.

Kafka soon experienced the first outward signs of the tuberculosis that would eventually kill him. He left for a holiday at the home of sister Ottilie in northwest Bohemia, where she lived and worked a farm with her husband, Josef David. Both the company and the setting seemed a healthy response to the disease. Periods at various sanatoriums would interrupt the pleasure of his sister's company by 1918.

---

[66] Enotes, The Great Wall of China, Franz Kafka – www.enotes.com/topics/great-wall-china

By 1919, Kafka was in northern Italy doing his best to heal and beginning a new romance with journalist and translator Milena Jesenska, a married woman. The relationship went as past ones had, with streams of letters and virtually no actual contact. Still, Kafka deemed her to be the second great love of his life. Following a series of love affairs, Jesenska's father had confined her in the Veleslavin Insane Asylum on grounds of "moral insanity." Despite her fascination with Kafka, she would not leave her husband, and the relationship ended as the others had, with a letter. Out of this "affair of the heart" came a publishable collection of *Letters to Milena*. She in return was the first to translate Kafka's works into a foreign language.

Around this time, Kafka attempted an autobiography of sorts. What emerged was entitled *Letter to His Father*. In this diatribe, he intended to vent every point of contention to the person he feared most in the world, and Kafka himself described it to Jesenska as "a lawyer's letter."[67] Others describe it as "a furious indictment."[68] Horrific memories range from being thrown outside for a night in the cold in return for requesting a glass of water to artificial and forced shows of faith. Amidst the other charges, Kafka openly questioned how his father could

---

[67] Eric Ormsby, Man and His Maker: Kafka's 'Letter to My Father', The New York Sun, July 9, 2008 – www.nysun.com/man-and-his-maker-kafkas-letter-to-my-father/814571/

[68] Eric Ormsby

criticize him for not making an effort at religion due to his own "insignificant scrap"[69] of authentic Judaism.

In the last of Kafka's great surrenders, his father never read the work because his son never sent it. Nothing was released or resolved, and readers are left only with the son's side of the conflict. In the work, Kafka recalled other such moments of failed courage, including a chance meeting with his father while strolling with friend Gustav Janouch. Hermann Kafka is said to have bellowed at his son, "Franz! Go home. The air is damp." Kafka whispered to his friend, "My father, he's worried about me…love often wears the face of violence."[70]

In Kafka's final summer, his time was spent writing "The Castle", based largely on the premise of "The Trial" several years earlier. The character K is summoned to the castle for an unknown purpose. Arriving in the village, he is generally unwelcome, and must seek permission from the Count to remain. Gaining access to the castle brings him in contact with two guards who know nothing but claim that no error has occurred because the castle's bureaucracy is perfect. K winds his way through a series of secretaries, but the story remains unfinished, with multiple endings possible. Childhood trauma, revitalized infantile fantasies, and institutional stalemates are all

------

[69] Matthew Roth

[70] Eric Ormsby

present in "The Castle". Brod believed that his friend, unable to find his purpose, was allowed to "wear himself out"[71] at the village in a punitive religious experience, and that he was to die by spending the last of his energy in the struggle. Christina Sizemore contended that of all the possibilities, the most unsettling element of K's summons to the castle is that there are "two irreconcilable interpretations of reality."[72] Anxious enough for the reader, the "interpretation" is for the character an in-the-moment crisis of unfamiliarity at odds with former expectations.

The other hallmark of Kafka's last year of life was one final romance. Dora Diamant, Jewish and hailing from Poland, was 20 years Kafka's junior. Emigrating to Germany to avoid family circumstances, she met the author at Müritz, a resort on the Baltic coast. Diamant served as a volunteer at the Jewish People's Home tending to the needs of eastern European refugees. Kafka was immediately fascinated, and unlike previous relationships, they moved in together. By the end of 1923, they were in Berlin, where the people were suffering through "alarming inflation and material hardship."[73] They could not afford electricity, heated food with candle ends, and

[71] Peter Dow Webster, A Critical Examination of Franz Kafka's "The Castle", *American Imago*, Vol 8, no. 1 (March, 1951), Johns Hopkins University Press.

[72] Christina W. Sizemore, Cognitive Dissonance and the Anxiety Response to Kafka's The Castle, *The Comparatist*, Vol. 4 (May, 1980), University of North Carolina Press

[73] Kafka Museum, Dora Diamant – www.kafkamuseum.cz/en/franz-kafka/women/dora-diamant/

were forced to move three times.

In early 1924, Kafka's health took a sudden downturn. He went alone to a sanatorium in Prague for a short period, after which he and Diamant moved to Austria together. There, they lived together for three months. Kafka was sent to the Wienerwald Sanatorium near Vienna, then to the laryngology clinic of Professor Hajek, and finally to Dr. Hoffmann's sanatorium in Klosterneuburg.

Even in failing health, Kafka and Diamant fantasized aloud about moving to Palestine, and eventually to Tel Aviv to open a Jewish restaurant together. Dora was to cook, while he would work as a waiter. During his final days, Diamant campaigned to improve his health through a regimen of neuropathic treatments, a vegetarian diet, and large quantities of pasteurized milk.

Kafka's stories remained dark in tone, but after falling in love with Diamant, she became the most authentic version of all his distant loves. His stories retained their darkness, but a new strain of "whimsy"[74] was apparent. Some of his last stories included "The Burrow" and "The Hunger Artist", which are at times "self-referential and self-mocking."[75]

---

[74] Matthew Roth

[75] Matthew Roth

Despite Kafka's first extended period of intimacy, he still expressed a dark view of women in general, observing, "Women are traps which lie in wait for men in order to drag them into the finite."[76] However, given the state of his dependency, the quip rings hollow at a time when Diamant shouldered the entirety of his care. Kafka approached death as an appropriate process for the growing artist. He posited that enlightenment is brought about by a "gradual disuse of the world,"[77] and that the "first sign of the beginning of understanding is the wish to die."[78]

Although the political tendencies of both Kafka and Diamant leaned toward socialism, the fervor for political revolution faded at the end. Kafka did not trumpet a breaking away or adherence to any system; in fact, he adroitly noted, "All revolutions evaporate leaving only the slime of a new bureaucracy."[79]

Reluctant to release his work to the public, Kafka requested that Brod, by this time his literary executor, destroy all his unpublished manuscripts. The same request was made to Diamant, but she and Brod both defied his wishes. She kept 20 notebooks of his writings and numerous private letters, all of which were confiscated by

---

[76] IMDB, Franz Kafka Biography – www.imdb.com/name/nm0434525/bio?ref=nm_ov_bio_sm
[77] IMDB
[78] IMDB
[79] IMDB

the Gestapo in 1933 and never recovered.

   Near the point of death, Kafka asked Diamant's rabbi father for permission to marry, but he was refused largely on the basis of his lack of depth as a loyal Jew. Nevertheless, Diamant stayed with him to the end, supplying all his needs and communicating with his family in "imperfect"[80] German. She cherished his memory over the following 30 years, and despite leaving many personal notes of her own, she published nothing about her former partner. She is said to have spoken at length of him on only one occasion.

   As his life came to an end, Kafka gave more ground to Judaism than he might ever have entertained as a younger man. In light of the author's early antagonism toward his heritage, Eli Kavon of *The Jerusalem Post* cites the presence of two Kafkas, one real and the other illusory. He suggested that there was a generic Kafka as perceived by the general public, and a Judaic Kafka who was devoted, albeit reluctantly, to his faith. In this equation, Kavon maintained that there never was such a thing as the generic Kafka, and that everything was Jewish. "A Report to an Academy", which was published in Martin Buber's Zionist journal, *Der Jude*, represented a general self-loathing in the Jewish community that fits Kafka to perfection. Like others of the faith, he yearned to achieve

---

⁸⁰ Kafka Museum, Dora Diamant

acceptance from the the majority culture. This, claims Kavon, is not the work of a universalist "generic" Jew. According to him, Kafka, despite his protestations, "lived as a Jew, and died much too early as a Jew."[81] He further insisted that Kafka's work represents the "ultimate act of assimilation."[82] Kafka's last observations on the subject faintly support such a notion, sadly musing that "the Messiah will come when he is no longer needed."[83]

Franz Kafka died of laryngeal tuberculosis on June 3, 1924 near Vienna at the age of 40. He had spent the last night of his life playing puppet shadow games with Diamant in the evening. Unable to eat, he then spent his final hours editing "The Hunger Artist". He was buried in the New Jewish Cemetery of Prague's Žižkov district.

[81] Eli Kavon, Franz Kafka: Jew, *The Jerusalem Post*, June 6, 2016 – www.jpost/.com/blogs/Past-Imperfect-Confronting-Jewish-History/Franz-Kafka-Jew-456061

[82] Eli Kavon

[83] IMDB

A picture of Kafka's grave

Life After Death

Jaroslav Róna's *Statue of Franz Kafka* in Prague

"The tremendous world I have inside my head, but how to free myself and free it without being torn to pieces. And a thousand times rather be torn to pieces than retain it in me or bury it. That, indeed, is why I am here, that is quite clear to me." - Kafka

In 1925, Brod published *Amerika* and "The Castle". Little had been published during Kafka's lifetime, and "The Metamorphosis" remains the best-selling of all his works. "The Hunger Artist" was published posthumously in the summer of 1924, immediately following Kafka's death, and Brod published "The Great Wall of China" 14 years after its creation. Many of Kafka's short stories, unfamiliar to the public in the early 20ᵗʰ century, reached iconic status by the mid-20ᵗʰ century.

Kafka's mother died in 1931, and his father died in 1934. "The Burrow" was published during this period, and the anecdotal account of Kafka and the Doll has remained popular. A tale in which he meets a little girl in the park who has lost her doll, he takes it upon himself to write regular letters to the girl from the absent doll, pleading, "Please do not mourn me. I have gone on a trip to see the world. I will write you of my adventures."[84] When Kafka eventually gives the girl a new doll, she notices the difference at once. However, he pulls out an attached letter written by the doll claiming, "My travels have changed me."[85] The girl grows up to find another note in a crevice of the doll telling her that everything loved will be lost, but that "love will return in a different form."[86]

Kafka's stories of powerlessness in the face of unseen institutional forces resonated strongly in the face of World War II, during which all three of his sisters died in Nazi concentration camps or Jewish ghettos. Communities in Eastern Europe also identified with the stories while under

---

[84] Mary Benatar, Psychotherapist, author, Kafka and the Doll: the Pervasiveness of Loss, *HuffPost,* December 3, 2011

[85] Mary Benatar

[86] Mary Benatar

the yoke of the Soviet Union. During this time, the use of a new term, "Kafkaesque," became chic in the literary world. In 1988, a handwritten manuscript of "The Trial" sold for $1.98 million, the largest amount ever paid for such a modern work. The buyer was a West German book dealer who believed it to be the most important work in 20th century German literature. His only comment was "Germany had to have it."[87]

Kafka's birthplace, Tower House (Zum Turm) on the crossroads of Maiselova and U. Radnice Streets, is today named Franz Kafka Square. The structure burned down, with only the house portal surviving, but a memorial was sculpted on the house's site by Karel Hladik. In 2005, the Franz Kafka Museum opened its doors in the Herget Brickworks Building of Lesser Town on the banks of the Vltava River. Although Kafka generally hid specific settings from the reader, the Vltava and some of its surrounding landmarks, such as the cathedral and the toll bridge, were recognizable. Although he seldom ventured too far out of Prague, he was able to transform most backdrops into settings of hybrid reality. Locations are employed metaphorically, therefore the precise setting was immaterial. However, those with which he was familiar was self-informing, with less chance of error. The Kafka Museum is divided into two sections, one named

---

[87] Biography, Franz Kafka

Existential Space, and the other Imaginary Topography. The first presents the manner by which Prague shaped the author's life, and the latter describes the process by which he depicts his city.

The enduring reputation of Franz Kafka has only partially suffered due to his inability to complete lengthy works and the intermittent blank spots of time in which he was not writing, but there are also questions of his relevancy to the 21st century, and whether the genre in which he excelled is necessary in the wake of the Cold War. In June 2013, Joseph Einstein discussed this point while mentioning the universal themes that Kafka's work addressed. He compared Kafka to great writers who are "impressed by the mysteries of life,"[88] adding that Kafka was "crushed by them."[89] In the author's world, "illogic becomes plausible, guilt goes unexplained…brutal punishment [is] doled out for no reason."[90] Such a description seems starkly relevant for any era. Gregor becomes an insect because he already was one, in the mode of millions of humans "scurrying from train to train, [and] town to town."[91] As a spokesperson for the human race, Kafka himself represents the "dissatisfaction"[92] of anyone who finds himself in such a position. In this status,

---

[88] David L. Ulin, *Los Angeles Times Book Critic*, Why Kafka Matters, June 24, 2013

[89] David. L. Ulin

[90] David L. Ulin

[91] David L. Ulin

[92] David L. Ulin

he is not necessarily a heroic figure, as his woes are largely his own fault, and the key lesson from many of his stories is that people are ultimately responsible for their fates. Kafka attempts to narrow his autobiographical critique to neutralizing universal conditions, but it is of no use. Taking his family struggles and interposing them on the modern world is an artistic version of passing the buck. It is undeniably true that his father was unduly strict if not tyrannical, but the frail emotional nature of the son caused him to live with it for 31 years. His manner of employment may have shifted from one company to another, but the dissatisfied insurance agent never left his dire situation until prompted by illness. With few exceptions, he strung a group of strong women along with his frailty, stood them up far short of the altar, then mourned his own loneliness and sense of incompletion. Kafka was not a philosopher or a traditional novelist. The works, long and short, were generally bad dreams put to paper, "merg[ing] realism with fantasy"[93] in the manner of all dream lives. He is not a hero standing firm against institutional tyranny, but fodder to be run over by it.

What Kafka's power is based on, at least in part, is his use of words that "pare language and experience down to the elemental,"[94] a condition which humans must confront in their most heightened moments. In his use of black

---

[93] Matthew Roth

[94] Pericles Lewis, Franz Kafka, Campus Press, Yale University – www.campuspress.yale.edu/modernismlab/franz-kafka/

humor, a "tightly-controlled self-effacing style and surreal scenarios,"[95] he becomes the emblem of lower humanity as a messenger. In his cross-cultural strivings, he describes his circumstance to being taught to speak, but in the process becoming alienated from human communities and unable to go back.

Ironically, the majority of Kafka's work spread throughout the world without his knowledge, "spurring a legacy that was never meant to endure."[96] At least in an external sense, he never wanted to be celebrated because being treated that way might have deprived him of his greatest literary weapons: resentment toward the world and himself. In all likelihood, he sensed that the manuscripts would not be burned as requested, and no one is certain whether he ever truly wanted that wish acted out. The only hint from his own thoughts reminded other Czech artists, particularly Brod, that "Prague doesn't let go of either you or me."[97]

Among the most comprehensive accounts of Kafka's life and work is *Kafka: The Years of Insight* by Reiner Stach. In an article on the lengthy tome written for the *London Review*, Rivka Galchen mentioned the body of notes possessed by those close to the author that illuminate

---

[95] Pericles Lewis

[96] Renée Reizman, "Franz Kafka" the Brand, Alive and Well in Prague, Literary Hub-www.lithub.com/franz-kafka-the-brand-alive-and-well-in-prague/

[97] Renée Reizman

some detail of his life in Prague. The documents are informative to the personal periphery of the published works, to the point that Galchen offered an entirely unfamiliar view of Kafka the man. In her view, his regular regimen of disasters, many self-inflicted, are comedic in nature. She compared Kafka to the television show *Blackadder,* featuring Rowan Atkinson and his propensity for self-sabotage. To a lesser degree, the habit of British characters caught in mini-disasters can also be seen in John Cleese's *Fawlty Towers*.

Such a view may not be merely a quirky British take on Kafka's worldview. The suitcase filled with notes belonging to the daughter of one of Brod's lovers supports the claim. Kafka was known to "laugh uncontrollably"[98] when reading his own works to friends. Having embarked on a "silence cure,"[99] the writing of notes to replace speech has been employed as a point of comedy in several major publications.

Some of Kafka's notes were of a serious nature, but fundraising appeals for injured soldiers were mixed with requests for watering the peonies if the recipient can find a moment to take care of it. In the midst of those notes, he

---

[98] Rivka Galchen, What Kind of Funny Is He?, London Review of Books, Vol. 36 No. 23, Review of Kafka: The Years of Insight by Reiner Stach – www.lrb.co.uk/the-paper/v36/n231/rivka-galchen/what-kind-0of-funny-is-he

[99] Rivka Galchen

also wrote turbid, strategic love letters. In his letters to Felice Bauer, Kafka attempted to coerce her into breaking it off so that he will not have to do it himself. In one, he confessed to her, "I often doubt that I am a human being."[100] When that fails to hit home, he mentioned his doctor, who allegedly suggested to him, "You can marry if you put on sufficient weight."[101] He followed that up by candidly admitting that he did not want to marry or eat. Within a five-year period, the two actually saw each other for a total of 18 scattered days, and during that time, Kafka was wooing Bauer's friend Grete Bloch. On another occasion during this time, Kafka was elated when an attractive young schoolgirl called out to him, smiling and waving. He walked away in euphoria before realizing that what she called him was "Jew."[102]

The underlying motivation with which to cure isolation in the moments when he was momentarily weary of it was to elicit affection, then disappoint it with his absence. On the face of it, this belies a case of high egotism. By the same token, although he is described as an asexual individual, that may relate more to an absence of confidence in an actual interaction. At a distance, he fully understood the power of sexuality, and he often employed a deft, artistically veiled form of it. He mixed that with

---

[100] Rivka Galchen

[101] Rivka Galchen

[102] Rivka Galchen

self-demolition in order to receive attention and then banish it. His later notes to Dora Diamant reek of the overwrought rhetorical gymnastics of the conflicted lover too afraid to step forward and declare it in action. In one, he wrote to her, "How long will you be able to stand it? How long will I be able to stand your standing it?"[103]

Some of Kafka's stories hint at the satirical components of Kafka's otherwise bleak life story. As an example, while the central character of "The Judgment" stands at the "Door of Law," a device that has been specifically created for him, the defendant never walks through it. Among his short stories is self-commentary ascribed to an Olympic swimmer for whom swimming is not really possible, therefore making him "the champion of the impossible." The brief offering is an extended quip at his own expense, "a remarkable reflection on social norms, subjectively, and the impossible."[104] Regardless of one's potential for accomplishment, the fear of drowning remains the swimmer's central truth, so he is "always out of his depth."[105]

Other self-directed observations regarding "the impossible" are legion, and Kafka seems ever in search of an improved manner of expressing it. In a related remark,

---

[103] Rivka Galchen

[104] E-flux Conversations, Kafka on Swimming and the Impossible – www.conversations.e-flux.com/t/kafka-on-swimming-and-the-impossible/10007

[105] E-flux Conversations

he likens himself to a "first-grader" who flunks the year eight times in succession. To him, the world is an individual who now resides in the eighth grade, "on the verge of an impossible graduation."[106] In another, he describes his inner self as being repeatedly struck by lightning as he nears the finish line. In short, nearly every example of Kafka's output is associated with hopeful transcendence, only to be derailed by an unseen and obscure entity, whether it is "the unreachable Sovereign, the inaccessible Law, a woman, or absent God."[107]

There are plenty of things about Kafka to credit and criticize, but it seems likely that his conflicted nature was necessary to produce the works he did. In a sense, Kafka seemed to understand that as well. As the legendary author aptly put it, "Don't bend, don't water it down, don't try to make it logical. Don't edit your own soul according to the fashion. Rather, follow your obsessions mercilessly."[108]

Online Resources

Other books about Kafka on Amazon

Further Reading

A Gentleman's Library, Amerika (Franz Kafka): A

---

[106] E-flux Conversations

[107] E-flux Conversations

[108] AZquotes, Franz Kafka – www.azquotes.com/author/7682-Franz-Kafka

Summary and Analysis – www.gentleman'slibrary.com/amerika-franz-kafka-summary-and-analysis/

AZ Quotes, Frank Kafka Quotes – www.azquotes.com/author/7682-Franz-Kafka

Benatar, May, Psychotherapist, author, Kafka and the Doll: The Pervasiveness of Loss, HuffPost, Dec. 3, 2016

Biography, Franz Kafka, Author, (1883-1924) April 2, 2014 – www.biography.com/writer/franz-kafka

Church, Margaret, Time and Reality in Kafka's The Trial and The Castle, Twentieth Century Literature Vol. 2 No. 2 (July 1956)

Cliff's Notes, The Metamorphosis and Other Studies, Summary and Analysis, The Judgment "(Das Urteil)" – www.cliffsnotes.com/literature/m/the-The Metamorphosis-and-otherstories/summary-and-analysis/the-judgment-das-urteil

E-flux Conversations, Kafka on Swimming and the Impossible – www.converatioins.e-flux.com/t/kafka-on-swimming-and-the-impossible

Enotes.com, The Great Wall of China, Franz Kafka – www.enotes.com/topic/great-wall-china

Fickert, Kurt J., A Literal Interpretation of "In the Penal

Colony," Modern Fiction Studies, Vol. 17, no. 1, Special Number the Modern German Novel (Spring, 1971) Johns Hopkins University Press

Fowler, Doreen F., "In the Penal Colony": Kafka's Unorthodox Theology, College Literature Vo. 6 No. 2, CEA Increment (Spring 1979) Johns Hopkins University Press

Franz Kafka, German Language Writer, Encyclopaedia Britannica – www.britannica.combiography/franz-kafka

Franz Kafka <Museum – www.kafkamuseum-cz/en/

Franz Kafka Museum, Franz Kafka, Assicurazioni Generali – www.kafkamuseum.cz/en/franz-kafka/employment/assicurazioni-generali/

Franz Kafka Museum, Felice Bauer – www.kafkamuseum.cz/franz-kafka/women/felice-bauer/

Franz Kafka – www.franzkafka-online.info-FranzKafka

Galchen, Rivka, What Kind of Funny Is He?, London Review of Books, Vol. 36 No. 23, Review of Kafka: The Years of Insight by Reiner Stach – www.lrb.co.uk/the-paper/v36/n231/rivka-galchen/what-kind-0of-funny-is-he

Guth, Hans P., Symbol and Contextual Restraint: Kafka's "Country Doctor" PMLA, Vol. 80 no. 4 (Sep., 1965) Modern Language Association

Haffner, Charlotte Yiddish Theater, Franz Kafka and Art Movements of the 20th Century, Jewish Museum London – www.jewishmuseum.org.uk/2018/1/11/yiddish-theater-franz-kafka-and-art-movements/

IMBB, Franz Kafka Biography – www.imbb.com/name/nm0434525/bio?ref=nm_or_bio_sm

Jewish Virtual Library, Czech Republic Virtual Jewish History Tour – www.jewishvirtuallibrary.org/czech-republic-virtual-jewish-history-tour

Kartinager, Donald M., Job and Joseph K.: Myth in Kafka's "The Trial", Modern Fiction Studies Vol. 8 No. 1, FRANZ KAFKA Special Number (Spring 1962), Johns Hopkins University Press

Kavon, Eli, Franz Kafka: Jew, the Jerusalem Post, June 6, 2016 – www.jpost.com//blogs/Past-Imperfect-Confronting-Jewish-History/Franz-KafkaJew-456061

Lewis, Pericles, Franz Kafka, Campus Press, Yale – www.campuspress.yale.edu/modernismlab/franz-kafka/

Life Persona.com, Who Was Franz Kafka/Life Works and Curiosities – www.lifepersona.com/who-was-franz-kafka-words-and-curiosities

Massimo, Guido, Franz Kafka's Vagabond Stars, Digital

Yiddish Theater Project – www.web.uwm.edu/yiddish-stage/fraqnz-kafkas-vagabond-stars

Mutual Inspiration Festival, 2014, Franz Kafka – www.mutualinspiration.org/2014/franz-kafka

Ormsby, Eric, Man and His Maker: Kafka's 'Letter to My Father', The New York Sun, July 9, 2008 – www.nysun.com/man-and-his-maker-kafkas-letter-to-my-father/814571/

Poem Hunter, Franz Kafka – www.poemhunter.com/franz-kafka/

Quora, What is Franz Kafka's Philosophy All About – www.quora.com/what-is-franz-kafakas-philosophy-all-about/

Reizman, Renee, "Franz Kafka" the Brand, Alive and Well in Prague, Literary Hub – www.lithub.com/franz-kafka-the-brand-alive-and-well-in-Prague/

Rolleston, James, Temporal Space: A Reading of Kafka's "Betrachtung", modern Austrian Literature, Vol. 11 no. ¾, Special Franz Kafka Issue (1978), Association of Austrian Studies

Roth, Matthew, Franz Kafka, the 20th Century's Realist Surrealist, Jewish Learning – www.myjewishlearning.com/article/franz-kafka/

Ryan, Judith, Kafka Before Kafka, The Early Stories, a Companion to the Works of Franz Kafka, NED-New Edition, 2002, Boydell and Brewer, Camden House.

Schaffner, Anna Katharina, Masochism: Franz Kafka and the Eroticization of Suffering, Springer – www.link.springer.com/chapter/10.1057/9780230358904_10

Shmoop, Franz Kafka Timeline – www.schmoop.com/franz-kafka,timeline.html

Sizemore, Christina W., Cognitive Dissonance and the Anxiety Response to Kafka's The Castle, The Comparatist, Vol. 14, (May 1980) University of North Carolina Press

Straus, Nina Pelikan, Transforming Franz Kafka's "The Metamorphosis", Signs, Vol. no. 3 (Spring 1989) University of Chicago Press

Thiher, Allen, Kafka's First Experiments in Writing Fiction, from Understanding Franz Kafka, 2018, University of South Carolina

Ulin, David L., Why Kafka Matters, Los Angeles Times Book Critic, June 24, 2013

Vitalis – Franz Kafka's World, Kafka's Illness – www.vitalis-verlag.com/en/topics/kafkas-world/kafkas-krankheit/

Webster, Peter Dow, A Critical Examination of Franz Kafka's "The Castle," American Imago, Vol. 8 No. 1 (March, 1951) Johns Hopkins University Press

Zilcosky, john, Kafka's Travels: Exoticism, Colonialism, and the Traffic of Writing, Reviewed by Christina Gerhardt, TRANSIT –
www.transit.berkely7.edu/2006/gerhardt/

Free Books by Charles River Editors

We have brand new titles available for free most days of the week. To see which of our titles are currently free, click on this link.

Discounted Books by Charles River Editors

We have titles at a discount price of just 99 cents everyday. To see which of our titles are currently 99 cents, click on this link.

www.ingramcontent.com/pod-product-compliance
Lightning Source LLC
Chambersburg PA
CBHW080723120726
48001CB00010B/3128